COLOUR J

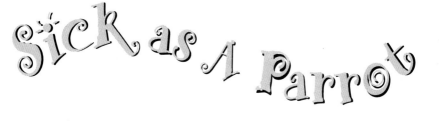

Sick as a Parrot

Michaela Morgan
and Trevor Dunton

Collins

COLOUR JETS

First published in Great Britain by
HarperCollins Publishers Ltd 1997

3 5 7 9 10 8 6 4

Text © Michaela Morgan 1997
Illustrations © Trevor Dunton 1997

The author and the illustrator assert the moral right to
be identified as the author and the illustrator of the work.

A CIP record for this title is available
from the British Library.

ISBN 0 00 675322 1

Printed in Printing Express Limited, Hong Kong

Chapter 1
The Sensible Sullivans

The Sullivans are a very sensible family.

Granny Sullivan sweeps and sorts.

A place for everything and everything in its place.

Mum dusts and polishes.

Spick and span, clean and shiny.

And then there's Dad. He likes to tidy and organise.

Soon have everything sorted!

Even the twins, Jake and Kate, are sensible. They have never lost a single sock in their lives and they keep their toys in alphabetical order.

A for Ape or M for Monkey?

So that Tuesday in June was a bit of a shock for them.

"Burglar perhaps," said Dad. "But what sort of a burglar takes silver spoons and bottle tops and leaves the video and the computer?"

"Magpie perhaps?" suggested Mum.

7

"Pirate actually," said a deep voice. "And afore ye start a-bellowing and a-billowing, you can have it all back if you just let me go

"Let me go! Let me go!" squawked another voice.

OOOO AARRGH!

Chapter 2
A Bulge in the Curtains

LET ME GO!

The voices were coming from the curtains, which had a suspicious pirate-shaped bulge in them.

Let me go!

At the bottom of the curtains, one salt-encrusted boot peeped out. Towards the top of the curtains was a pointy beak shape.

Mum just tutted and pulled the curtains back.

There, with his wooden leg out of the open window, was a burly, bearded pirate.

He offered to shake his hook with Gran.

Short Bob Silver's the name. Pleased to meet you.

She just sniffed. He didn't look like their sort of person at all.

Short Bob Silver was not neat and tidy in the least. He seemed to have mislaid several bits of his body rather carelessly.

And he did not look sensible at all.

The Sullivans stared at him in disbelief.
He had a wild and desperate look in his
one eye. He had a scruffy, balding parrot
on one shoulder. And he had a fierce dog
holding on to his one good leg.

The dog was Rover, the Sullivan family pet. His teeth were stuck into the pirate's trouser leg and he wasn't letting go.

"Good dog, Rover," said Dad. "You've got him trapped."

"You can have it all back," growled Short Bob.

"All back," echoed the parrot.

"Just let me go!" pleaded the pirate.

"Lemme go!" the bird agreed.

So the Sullivan family took all their stuff
back and told Rover to let go.

But he didn't.

He wouldn't.

Chapter 3
Sick as a Parrot

Gran fetched her sewing scissors and snipped a hole in the pirate's trouser leg. This made him look scruffier than ever.

"Poor Rover," said Jake.

"Poor Rover!" snorted Short Bob. "What about poor me?"

"You deserve it," said Dad, sternly.

You're a disgrace, stealing other people's belongings.

"It was just a few pieces of silver," said the pirate.

"Pieces of silver," echoed the parrot.

I was desperate.

Desprit!

It was or my poor parrot.

Poor parrot...

19

The Sullivans were beginning to feel sorry for this pathetic pirate.

"I've been an honest pirate, till now," whimpered Short Bob. "But my poorly parrot needs help and I need money to pay the vet…"

"I'm desperate to find a cure for my faithful, feathered friend," sighed Short Bob. "This 'ere parrot is very sick."

"Sick," repeated the parrot, and he sighed too.

"Poor thing," said Kate.

"Poor thing," the parrot agreed, and put his head under his wing.

Chapter 4
Gran to the Rescue

"What have you been feeding him?" asked Gran.

"The usual," said Short Bob. "Scraps o' this and scraps o' that. Oh, and this special medicine that I still owe the vet for."

DR NASTY'S PARROT CURE

Jake sniffed the medicine.
It was thick and green and
gloppy, and very unpleasant.
And it smelt like…

Gran peered at the parrot. "It's half starved, poor thing," she said. "I know about birds. They need to eat grain and seed or else they go…"

Nuts?

"Can't bear to see a poor, helpless creature suffering," said Gran. "Leave that parrot with me. I'll soon have him sorted."

And that's how a sensible family like the
Sullivans came to have a parrot
living in their bathroom.
(Gran thought the steam
and heat would
perk it up.)

And that's why they also ended up with
a pirate in the attic.

I've loved that bird since he was an egg. If he's staying, so am I.

Chapter 5
Home Sweet Home

Short Bob Silver soon made himself at home.

He made a few things for his room.

Nautical but nice!

Did a bit of painting and decorating.

Soon have this shipshape.

BOB'S CABIN

Helped with the washing…

…and the shopping.

He was particularly good at cleaning and babysitting.

Baby Sullivan loved being looked after by the pirate. Short Bob would rock him in a hammock, tell him tall tales and sing sea shanties.

He even liked changing nappies.

What shall we do with the dirty nappy?
What shall we do with the dirty nappy?
What shall we do with the dirty nappy?
       Early in the morning.

Peel it off and stuff it in a bucket.
 Peel it off and stuff it in a bucket.
  Peel it off and stuff it in a bucket.
       Early in the morning.

Clean 'im up and dry 'im nicely.
 Clean 'im up and dry 'im nicely.
  Clean 'im up and dry 'im nicely.
       Early in the morning.

Yo-ho-ho and powder his bum!

Chapter 6
A Pirate's Life for Them

"I don't know how we
ever managed without him,"
said Mum one day. Living with a
rough, tough pirate was turning out to
be a rather refreshing experience.

After only a few days, the sensible Sullivans were climbing and clambering, swinging, singing and yo-ho-ho-ing better than Short Bob Silver himself.

This pirate life's a proper tonic.

"I feel years younger," whooped Gran.

But the Sullivans weren't the only ones changing. Short Bob was becoming neater and tidier and more sensible by the minute.

Soon he had a well-brushed beard, gleaming teeth and a clean hanky. Not to mention a shiny polished wooden leg, a sparkling hook and clean underpants.

The problem was the parrot. It had perked up a bit with Gran's care, but it was still pretty seedy.

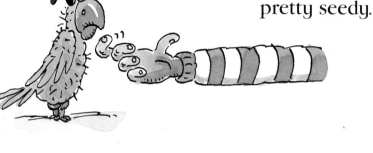

Every day, more and more feathers dropped out.

Underpants.

It spent most of the day dozing in the corner, waking from time to time to mutter something rude, then nodding off again.

"We've tried everything," sighed Mum. "If we don't cure it soon, it will be completely bald and then it won't be able to fly."

Kate knew all about parrots now. She'd borrowed every book she could find in the library.

A picture of a featherless parrot had filled her with horror.

ENCYCLOPEDIA OF PARROT AILMENTS

PROFESSOR DICK E. BIRD

We can't let this poor parrot end up like that!

But what could they do?

They tried giving it healthy food.

It's called a fruity sundae.

sigh

The parrot just looked at it and sighed.

They tried teaching it keep fit.

...and 1 and 2 and 1 and 2...

The parrot wouldn't even try.

They'd already tried keeping it in a hot
and steamy rain-forest-type place
(the bathroom).

The parrot just got damp.

Short Bob sang to it and tickled it
and told it tall tales:

– but nothing worked.

As he watched his faithful, feathered friend fading away, big blobby tears crept down Short Bob's hairy cheek. They splashed on to the parrot, who just got damper.

Chapter 7
Something Turns Up

One afternoon, to take their minds off the parrot, the Sullivans helped Short Bob move some more of his belongings into their house.

Well, shiver me timbers. It's ole ol' shark Monty.

What a mess they were! Dusty, tattered, untidy! In no order at all!

The Sullivan family couldn't wait to get
tidying and dusting and sorting.

One by one, long lost pirate belongings were turned up by Gran's relentless organising.

There certainly were a lot of papers.
There were:

treasure maps

vet bills (lots!)

Rum & biscuit souffle
YOU WILL NEED
1 BOTTLE RUM
A LOT OF EGGS
MORE RUM
SHIPS BISCUITS

PIRATES 'R' US
Cutlass ---- £2
Hanky ---- 60p
Dirty fingernail
polish ---- 80p
Extra hard
toilet paper --- 40p

JIM
the
VET

BILL
~~
~~
~~
~~
~~   2.00
~~   4.50
~~   2.00
~~   8.00
           1.50
TOTAL ---- 18.00
LATE

Shark Fri
Ingredients
1 shark
3 onions
7 old socks
1 large

DOG + EYE P
LUNCH
BAKED BEA
TOAST

STREET MA
OF CROYDON

THIS IS TO CERTIFY
That
Short Bob Silver
HAS COMPLETED
100m
DOGGY PADDLE

BILL
~~
~~
~~
TOTAL
VERY
LATE   13.0
            3.50
            43.00

tha
unless th
is paid by next
Tuesd·   will
have   LAUNDRY
but   LIST

100
SWASHBU
WAUG W
HA

swimming
certificates

old bus tickets

recipes and fashion tips

44

And this very
interesting book.

PET HINTS FOR PIRATES

Chapter 1

HOW TO TREAT YOUR SCURVY DOG

Chapter 2

A SHARK IS NOT AN IDEAL PET

Chapter 3

HOW TO PERK UP YOUR PARROT

"Ooh!" said Gran, and she turned to Chapter 3.

Chapter 3
HOW TO PERK UP YOUR PARROT

Is your parrot down at beak? Feathers ruffled? Bedraggled? Sulky? Depressed?

Then try this instant Parrot Perk-up.

You will need:
Bananas, baked beans, lemonade, coconut, black pepper, Extract of Bat, Essence of Rat, seven fat fleas, a glass of rum, a teaspoon of chilli, plenty of fruit and nut chocolate, a sherbet fountain and a splash of sea water.

> Ooo-ar! I wonder if that belonged to my great-grand daddy. Or my great-great-grand daddy. Or my great-great-great-grand daddy. Or...

"No one's that great," said Gran crisply. "I think we should try this out. See if it works. We'll need a guinea pig."

"But I 'aven't got a guinea pig," sighed Short Bob. "All I got is this 'ere bird."

"I'll explain it to you later, dear," said Gran, tutting. "Right now I've got to go shopping. I'm off."

> I'm off...

Chapter 8
Recipe for Success?

In no time at all (considering how difficult it is to find Essence of Rat in Tesco) Kate, Jake and Gran were holding a bowl full of interesting titbits in front of the jaded parrot.

Rats!

"Try a bit," urged Kate. "We've all worked hard on this. We're all…"

"Now, just be sensible, dear, and have a beak of this…" said Gran, fishing out a piece of coconut.

"Maybe you should try a port and starboard attack," suggested Short Bob, nautically.

So Kate forced some sherbet and pepper into the parrot's unwilling beak on the left (port) side, while Jake squashed in some baked beans, lemonade and a bit of bat on the right (starboard).

"Avast there!" said Dad (speaking piratically). "Time for the sea water."

He aimed a bucketful at the miserable bird.

sea Water... errgh!!!

"Stand well back now," shouted Gran.

And just as well. Because the parrot began to perk up.

First he opened
one bleary eye
and sighed in
his usual weary way.

SIGH!

Where am I?

HIC!

Then he
hiccuped and
jumped.

He began
to fizz and
pop.

POP

POP

POP

Then he gave a particularly large pop and fell beak first into the bowl of parrot perk-up.

First he just lay there, opening and closing his beak, and blinking. Then…

"Chocs away!" squawked the parrot and fairly whizzed around the room.

Hiccuping and burping and making little popping noises, there was just no stopping him.

Short Bob Silver beamed.

The parrot perched and preened.

His
feathers
shone.

His beak
glowed.

Then the parrot zoomed off again.

He whizzed and whirled.

supersonic!

He looped the loop.

What a tonic!

Then he
dive-bombed
back into
the bowl,
screeching
and
squawking,
singing and
talking.

Down
down,
deeper
and down.

Why, he even started
to tap dance!

He was a truly perked-up parrot.

"Well, that seems to have done the trick," said Gran, coming in with tea and chocolate cake. "I'm sure your vet would buy a recipe like that. I reckon your bill's paid."

"Bill's paid! Bill's paid!" whooped the parrot. He'd never liked being in debt.

"Vet's name's Jim, not Bill," said the pirate, "but I reckon you do be right."

If 'e don't take this 'ere Parrot Perk-up as payment, my name's not Short Bob.

Which it is.

"Parrot power!" squawked the parrot,
who was now full of beans (not to
mention fruit and nut chocolate,
lemonade and sherbet).
He perched on
Gran's head.

Who's a
pretty girl,
then?

Gran blushed. "Who'd like a bit of chocolate cake, then?" she asked.

"Aye," continued the pirate. "I do be wantin' a bit of that there cake and then I do be wantin'…"

He stood still and sniffed the air.

. . . I do be wantin' the smell of salt water. It's worked wonders for me parrot and it'll work wonders for me.

Wonderful me!

It be time for me to set sail again.

The Sullivans gasped.

"O'course, yer all could come too," said Short Bob, "but yer all too sensible to sail the seven seas with an ol' pirate like me… aren't you?"

"All aboard then!" said the pirate. "All aboard!"

"All aboard," said the parrot, and with one happy burp he flapped his shiny, many-coloured wings, took flight and led the way.

THE ~~END~~ Stern